A Little Girl in a Big, Big World

by
**Daijha Cain,
Ashley Cooper, and
Makayla Harris**

Illustrated by
Nathaniel Oliver

Reach Incorporated | Washington, DC
Shout Mouse Press

Reach Education, Inc. / Shout Mouse Press
Published by
Shout Mouse Press, Inc.
www.shoutmousepress.org

Copyright © 2015 Reach Education, Inc.
ISBN-13: 978-0996927437 (Shout Mouse Press, Inc.)
ISBN-10: 0996927433

Dedicated to young black girls
all over the world.
We want you to know
that you can make a change
in your community.

My name is Jasmine and I'm 8 years old.

I want to make a difference in my world.
But how?

I love school and I love to flow.
But sometimes, you know,
life gives you such a blow.

I just feel like a little girl in a big, big world.

Every day on my way to school,
    I see people sitting on the corner.
    They beg for money.
    They shake their cups.
    One man calls out to us:
    "Can y'all give me something so I can eat?"

    But people walk past and just shake their heads.
    "Hey!" I say. "I know y'all see this man."

    It makes me feel some type of way.
    I feel bad. I feel sad. I feel mad.

                    I feel like a little girl in a big, big world.

Every day on my way to school,
   I see teenagers with empty bookbags.

   "Where you going, Little Ma?"
   "I'm going to school, somewhere you should be," I say.
   "School's for squares," they say.
   "I'm a triangle. I'm different."
   "What's that supposed to mean?" They laugh.
   "If you went to school you'd know what I'm talking
   about," I say.
   "You're so little and we're so big, you can't tell us what
   to do."

I feel like a little girl in a big, big world.

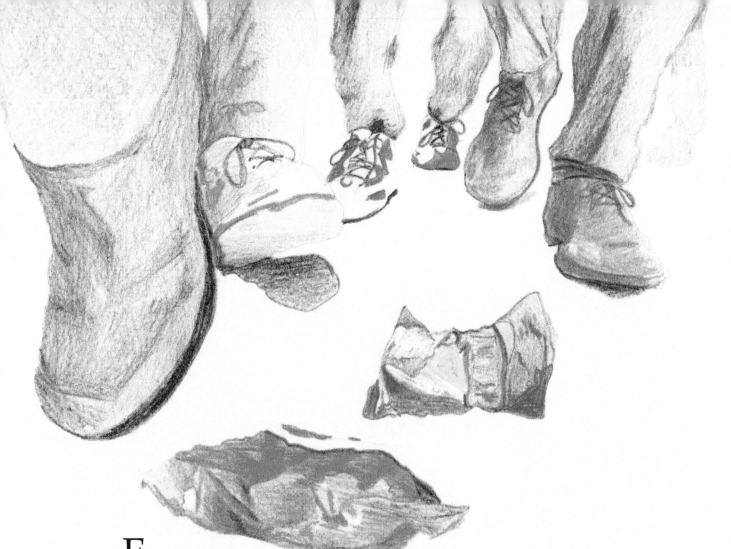

Every day on my way home from school, I see people
dropping trash right on the ground. They drop candy
wrappers, and soda bottles, and Doritos bags.

"Who do you think you are," I say, "Hansel and Gretel?"

They walk past me like they can't hear a word.
I try to speak louder. They move their heads like,
Where's that noise coming from?

"Down here!" I say. "How's the weather up there?
Anyways, you're littering."
"Whatever," they say,
and the papers flutter around me to the ground.
If you just paid attention, I think,
the little things can make a big difference.
But maybe I'm too little to make any difference at all.

I feel like a little girl in a big, big world.

One day I'm walking home.
There's trash everywhere. Gum gets stuck to my shoes.

I pick up my little brother at the bus stop.
His name is JJ, and he's even littler than me.

I hold his hand as he skips down the sidewalk.
He bends down and picks up a crumpled piece of paper.

"LeBron James!" he says,
and tries to shoot it in the trash can.

We keep walking and we see more and more papers on the ground. I start to get annoyed.

"Stop, JJ," I say. "If you want to help, just pick these up with me and we can put them in the recycling bin."

As I reach up to dump them in the bin, one falls out.

I wonder, *What does this paper say, anyways?*

I pause for a minute and think.
I want to go to a big theater and finally be famous.

But I'm little.

Nobody listens to me.
Adults won't listen to me.
Kids won't listen to me.
Even JJ is too busy being LeBron to listen to me now.

I feel like a little girl in a big, big world.

When I get home, I walk upstairs.
My room is covered in posters of rappers:
Nicki Minaj, Tunechi, Larry the Camel.
In my spare time, I like to make my own beats.

I turn around and face the mirror. I look at myself.
I didn't get any bigger.
Sigh.

"You know you're never going to change anything,
right?" says a voice near my ear.

I look up.
It's a Mini-Me above my shoulder!
She's wearing fat daddies and my purple shirt.
She looks so sad.

Then I hear another voice.

"You're going to be big like me if you keep on doing what you're doing," she says.

It's a Bigger-Me on my other shoulder!
She's carrying a boom box and smiling.
She looks so much happier.

I step away from the mirror and look left and right, but they're gone.

I think about what makes me feel good about myself.
And then I finally come to a decision.

I guess that I should…

I find myself walking into a crowded room with a stage. I don't know if I can do it. But I'm going to try.

The crowd is calm, but there's a ton of people.
"Where's the next performer?" I hear someone say.
They still can't see me.
I wave my hands around.
"Down here!"
Everybody laughs, but somebody passes me the mic.
I clear my throat.

"This rap is dedicated to the problems we have in our community," I say. "Drop the beat, DJ."

I look around at my community
I wanna make a change
I see a homeless guy
Asking for some change

If that was you on the corner
It wouldn't be so funny
We gotta help the homeless
Give that man some money

It's 8:45 and these kids not in school
They standing on the block, try'na look cool
Little do they know, they look like a fool

That's my little brother
You gotta teach 'em young
When he takes a shot
He sticks out his tongue

At least he's pickin' trash up
It's a clean way to ball
And y'all should help us out
'Cause we feelin' kinda small

Take PRIDE in yo' hood
I don't mean to give a speech
Just like you clean your room
You gotta clean the streets

Take PRIDE in yourself
Don't let your future burn
You gotta go to class
You gotta wanna learn

Give PRIDE to the people
Don't dismiss who they are
If we support one another
We can take each other far

I love all my people
I love my community
But before things can change
It starts with you and me

As I finish, I see the audience nodding their heads.
They must really like my rap, I think.

Then JJ looks up at me.
"Dang, Little Ma, you HUGE," he says.
The crowd roars.

I'm feeling good.
Finally, people get what I was trying to tell them.
I just had to be confident and stop doubting myself.
I had to push through.

JJ goes up to the DJ and whispers something to him.
Then the music starts and we know what to do...

Two days later, my alarm wakes me up with Beyonce singing, "I woke up like this..." I start to sing along.

As I'm on my way to school, a group of ladies I saw at the open mic call out to me.

"Hey there, Jasmine. I been thinking about your rap the other night."

"Thank you. You look out for the community, all right?"

I keep walking and
I don't see the same
group of boys
hanging out on
the corner.

*Man, I hope they're
in school,* I think.

I round the bend
and I don't have
gum on my shoe.

I even see a little boy
picking up some trash.

I look his way and smile.

And then I see
the homeless guy.
A man on his way to
work stops to talk and
doesn't just ignore him.
He gives him a dollar, too.

Finally, people are
giving back!

I smile.
All theses changes
are happening because
I spoke my mind.

You know I don't wanna
toot my own horn, but
TOOT TOOT TOOT!

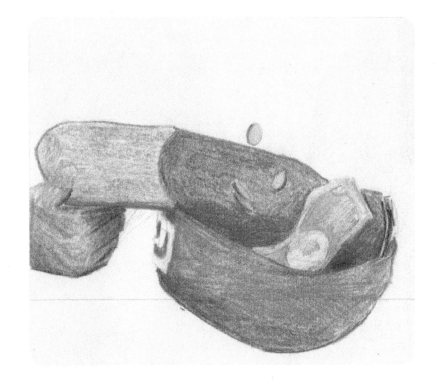

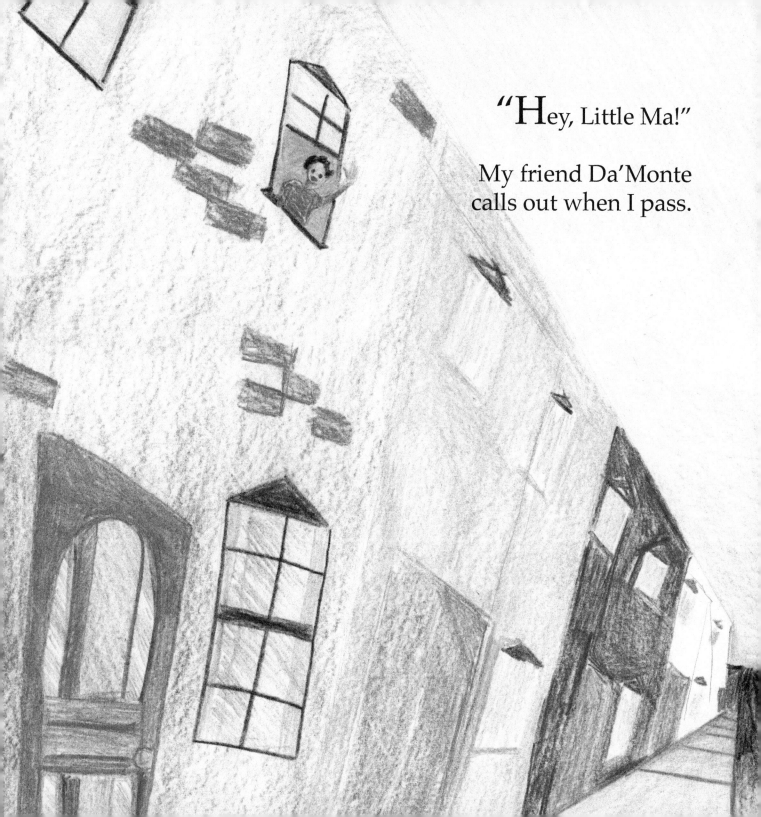

"Hey, Little Ma!"

My friend Da'Monte
calls out when I pass.

"Who you calling 'Little?'" I say.

"I'm a Big, Big Girl
in a brand NEW world."

About the Authors / Illustrator

DAIJHA CAIN
is a student at Eastern Senior High School in Washington, DC. Daijha loves to write, act, and sing. She is currently an employee at Reach Incorporated and is 15 years old. This is her first children's book.

MAKAYLA HARRIS
is 14 years old and is a proud student of McKinley Technology High School. Her favorite subjects are math and writing. She enjoys working with little kids, and she has been with Reach for a year. This is her first children's book.

ASHLEY COOPER
is 17 years old and attends Ballou Senior High School in DC. Her dream is to be a producer and an R&B singer and one day to perform at the BET Awards. She is also a great athlete. This is her second children's book. Her first book, *The Hoodie Hero,* came out in 2014.

NATHANIEL OLIVER
is a painting major at the Rhode Island School of Design. He enjoys creating art through a variety of mediums: drawing, painting, photography, graphic design, sculpting, and printmaking. He also enjoys writing poems and short stories. Nathaniel is a graduate of DC's Duke Ellington School of the Arts.

D'JUAN THOMAS, RACHEL PAGE, and "SULLY" MULUGETA served as Story Scribes for this book.
KATHY CRUTCHER served as Story Coach and Series Editor.

Books by TEENS

Acknowledgments

For the third summer in a row, teens from Reach Incorporated were issued a challenge: compose original children's books that will both educate and entertain young readers. Specifically, these teens were asked to create inclusive stories that reflect the realities of their communities, so that every child has the opportunity to relate to characters on the page. And for the third summer in a row, these teens have demonstrated that they know their audience, they believe in their mission, and they take pride in the impact they can make on young lives.

Twelve writers spent the month of July brainstorming ideas, generating potential plots, writing, revising, and providing critiques. Authoring quality books is challenging work, and these authors have our immense gratitude and respect: Rochelle, Destiney, Naseem, Darrin, Artrise, Aderemi, Taijah, Litzi, Makayla S., Ashley, Daijha, and Makayla H.

These books represent a collaboration between Reach Incorporated and Shout Mouse Press, and we are grateful for the leadership provided by members of both teams. From Reach, D'Juan Thomas, Maggie Pahos, Dominique Beaudry, and Selamawit "Sully" Mulugeta acted as story scribes, working closely with authors to capture and develop their ideas. We simply wouldn't have been able to do it without our incredible Summer Program Director, Jusna Perrin.

From the Shout Mouse Press team, we thank story scribes Annie Rosenthal, Barrett Smith, and Rachel Page for bringing both fun and insight to the project. We can't thank enough illustrators Nathaniel Oliver, Cassie Paris, Leslie Pyo, and Zoe Gatti for bringing these stories to life with their beautiful artwork. We are grateful for the time and talents of these writers and artists!

Finally, we thank those of you who have purchased books and cheered on our authors. It is your support that makes it possible for these teen authors to engage and inspire young readers. We hope you smile as much while you read as these teens did while they wrote.

Mark Hecker,
Reach Incorporated

Kathy Crutcher,
Shout Mouse Press

About Reach Incorporated

Reach Incorporated develops grade-level readers and capable leaders by preparing teens to serve as tutors and role models for younger students, resulting in improved literacy outcomes for both.

Founded in 2009, Reach recruits high school students to be elementary school reading tutors. Elementary school students average 1.5 grade levels of reading growth per year of participation. This growth – equal to that created by highly effective teachers – is created by high school students who average more than two grade levels of growth per year of program participation.

As skilled reading tutors, our teens noticed that the books they read with their students did not reflect their reality. As always, we felt the best way we could address this issue was to let our teen tutors author new books. Through fanciful stories with diverse characters, our books invite young readers to explore the world through words. By purchasing our books, you support student-led, community-driven efforts to improve educational outcomes in the District of Columbia.

Learn more about all our books at www.reachincorporated.org/books.

About Shout Mouse Press

Shout Mouse Press is a nonprofit writing program and publishing house for unheard voices.

Founded in 2014, Shout Mouse partners with other nonprofit organizations serving communities in need and designs book projects that amplify the voices of those they serve. These books in turn amplify the missions of our nonprofit partners by creating tangible, marketable products that tell the story of their work and innovate their outreach and fundraising.

Through writing workshops designed for all levels of literacy, Shout Mouse coaches writers to tell their own stories in their own voices and, as published authors, to be agents of change in their communities. Shout Mouse authors have produced original children's books, memoir collections, and novels-in-stories.

Learn more and see our full catalog at www.shoutmousepress.org.

CPSIA information can be obtained at www.ICGtesting.com
Printed in the USA
BVOW07s0812260116

434212BV00002B/8/P